THE GARDEN PLANNER

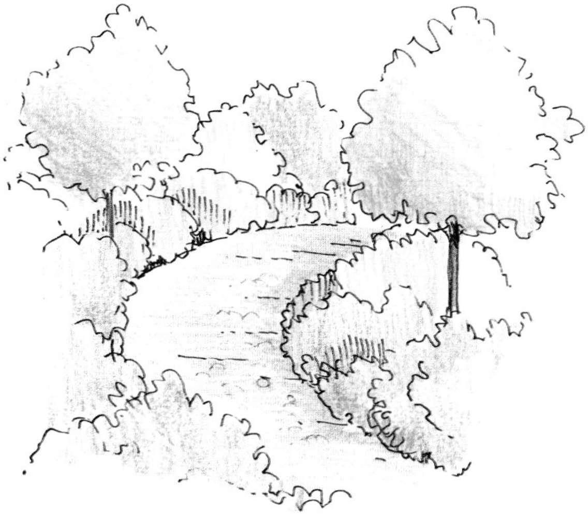